...cate this book to my mother, Alvenia.

She inspired me to write about the lack of historical information she learned in school during the 1960s as it related to ancient African studies and African American history. She grew up in an era that had heightened political, racial, and social tensions. As a result, she learned very little about African American accomplishments through her history textbooks.

I hope to inspire young readers today to become lifelong learners who develop a thirst for knowledge that encourages them to investigate and research historical events that might not be taught in their classrooms.

Sing along with Ashanti,
"I want to know my history,
I want to know all about me!"

Copyright © 2021 by Tanika Vellucci

All rights reserved. No part of this publication may be reproduced, distributed, or transmitted in any form or by any means, including photocopying, recording, or other electronic or mechanical methods, without the prior written permission of the publisher, except in the case of brief quotations embodied in critical reviews and certain other noncommercial uses permitted by copyright law.

Editors: Jane De Roussan and Carrie Jones.
Translator: Maylen Martinez

ISBN: 978-0-578-98507-7

First Printing, 2021
www.HayleysDoodles.com

ASHANTI AND KAMARI

Unlocking Their Past

by
Tanika Vellucci

pictures by
Hayley Moore

When Ashanti was a little girl, her grandparents told her she was special and gave her a gold necklace with a locket in the shape of a cowrie seashell. She did not know what that meant, but she knew it was important.

She learned that the meaning of her name is "thankfulness." It comes from the ancient African kingdom of Ghana. When she found out the historic meaning of her name linked her to Ghana and her ancestors, she knew why she felt special.

She began to have amazing dreams about the past. That is her wonder gift. Her dreams are vivid, and they are real. She knows she has to share them with her little brother. From then on through her dreams, Ashanti and Kamari travel back in time. They learn about the history of so many awesome people from the past.

"Ashanti, Ashanti, wake up!" shouts Kamari as he bangs on his sister's door.

"It's time for breakfast and Mom and Dad said that we can go to the museum after we eat. Please hurry!" Kamari begs.

Ashanti puts her pillow over her head as she tries to block the sunlight from hitting her eyes. There is another knock at her door five minutes later.

Kamari sits with his ear pressed against the outside of her door. Now he can hear exactly when his sister steps out of bed. Knock, knock.

Ashanti does not answer. She rolls over and grabs her cellphone off her nightstand. Still excited over the novelty of receiving her first cellphone on her twelfth birthday, Ashanti enjoys being able to talk to her friends when they are not in school.

Completely ignoring her brother, she checks to see if her best friend, Candace, sent her a text message after they left school yesterday.

"Okay, Ashanti, I will see you when you are awake." Kamari shrugs his shoulders as he scratches the top of his head.

Kamari has the most adorable curls, but he prefers their dad to cut his hair short so that he does not have to comb his hair as often. He heads downstairs to play with his favorite car set.

About fifteen minutes go by and Ashanti is finally awake. She stands up and takes a long stretch.

"Boy, Kamari wakes up with a lot of energy. Then again, what else do seven-year-olds do?" she mumbles as she recalls Kamari knocking on her door at 6:30! And on a Saturday morning!

She goes to the mirror over her dresser and takes off her silk scarf, rubbing her fingers across her braids. Rays of sunlight peek through the blinds and highlight the little, brown streaks in her dark, curly hair. Though her hair is braided back in cornrows, soft curls form around the edge of her face and at the end of each braid. She tries to straighten out each end. Ashanti has a beautiful complexion. It is like caramel with its hint of spice and honey

As she gathers her braids into one ponytail, she gazes into the mirror and remembers her mother's words.

"Ashanti has the most remarkable eyes. They are shaped like big, black crystal marbles."

Perhaps it's a mystical feature she embodies.

As Ashanti starts down the stairs, her mother is playing music and Ashanti instantly recognizes the voice of her favorite singer.

> "I want to know my history.
> I want to know all about me!"

Ashanti immediately finds pep in her step as she snaps her fingers, bops up and down, and moves her shoulders from side to side. The rhythm, the beat, sound, and lyrics of her favorite artist wake her up for good and a huge smile comes across her face. Caught up in the melody, she thinks about sharing the dream she had last night with her little brother.

Her mother snaps her fingers and sings along in the kitchen as well.

"I want to know my history...!"

"Good morning, sweetheart!" says Ashanti's mother as she kisses her on the forehead and hands her a plate of hotcakes with fresh fruit.

"Good morning, Mom. Thank you. Breakfast smells really good!" Ashanti replies. "Where's Dad?" She heard his voice earlier this morning while she was still in bed.

"He made your breakfast and then ran to the store to get a few parts for Kamari's car set. Looks like the battery is not working on his Hummer and remote. He will be back soon because we are planning to go to the museum after lunch," explains Ashanti's mother.

Instantly, Ashanti locks eyes with her brother, who is saturating his food with syrup while grinning from ear to ear. She walks away from her mother with her plate in hand.

Ashanti sits down at the table and gives him "that look" with her eyes wide open and eyebrows stretched so high.

"Kamari, I had another dream last night," she whispers. "I dreamt I was in a faraway land that was really hot, and there were lots of animals. You know, the kind we see at the zoo, but I was not at the zoo! There were giraffes, mountain nyalas, rhinoceroses, Menelik's bushbucks, gelada baboons, and black lions. So many of the animals, I have never seen before or even heard of. All the animals were friendly and they even talked. Then, suddenly, I was going to be carried off on a chariot to meet the king and queen. Oh, Kamari, it was absolutely beautiful!" says Ashanti, her face glowing.

Kamari stops drenching his plate and stares at his sister with eyes the size of big, brown saucers. He looks up with sheer amazement. "Gelada, gelada baboon. What in the world is that?" He asks.

Kamari gasps as he places the
half empty bottle of syrup on the table.

"So what happened? What happened next on your adventure? Who was the king and who was the queen? Where did they come from? Where did they live? Where were you? I want to know more!"

"Well, I'm not sure. It must have been somewhere in Africa. It was so hot, and I know giraffes live in the savannas of Africa," Ashanti explains.

"Wait a minute!" Kamari shouts. "Did you say kings and queens? There were no kings or queens in Africa except for in Egypt—our Black ancestors were only slaves! Mr. Smith taught us about kings, queens, and castles in Europe, but not in Africa. You must have your dream all mixed up because it does not make any sense. You've lost me," Kamari says confidently as he folds his arms and leans back in his chair.

"Kamari, do you remember when Grams and Gran-Gran went to Ethiopia last year? When they came back, they told us stories about their trip."

"Well, kind of ... but I only paid attention when they talked about the food they ate and the toys they brought back for me," says Kamari, grinning at his sister. "I must have tuned everything else out. Their stories are way too long and sometimes boring."

"There you go. You do not remember because you are always too busy being a spoiled brat! Anyway, while they were on their trip, they visited a town called **Aksum.**"

Kamari uncrosses his arms and draws in closer to listen with great intent. Ashanti closes her eyes in a state of deep concentration and then finally shouts out.

"Wait, wait a minute,"

Ashanti says as she frantically shakes her head. "I think my dream is coming back to me. Yes! I dreamt that I was in the ancient kingdom of Aksum!" she exclaims.

"I remember standing in front of a very tall stone object. It was just like the one we have in the living room. Except it was not small. It was huge. It was so tall that it appeared to stretch all the way into the sky and touch the clouds." Ashanti recalls.

Back to her dream, Ashanti tells her brother about a young girl that she saw walking alongside a mountainous grassy area.

"Her skin was that of copper and glowed as if she had been out in the sun from the day she was born. She was dressed in a simple but beautiful white dress," she tells him.

Ashanti remembers the girl's every move as the girl gracefully raised her arm to feed acacia leaves to a nearby giraffe. On each arm the girl wore gold bracelets with blue beads. The color of the beads signified the sky and energy.

Her hair was dark and wavy, braided very similarly to Ashanti's. Around her neck, she wore a layered golden necklace that signified sheer elegance and wealth.

"Wow! She is so pretty," Ashanti said to herself in her dream as she watched every move the girl made.

"Look Aida, Ashanti has finally arrived," said the giraffe as he lowered his head and began to wiggle his ears

with excitement.

He stuck out his gigantic, black tongue to embrace each tasty green leaf. Just then, Aida glanced over her shoulder to see Ashanti and smiled.

Luckily for Ashanti, she is always able to communicate with people in her dreams because they always speak English.

"Hello, excuse me. Can you please tell me where I am? But more importantly, did that giraffe just talk?" asked Ashanti in a skeptical voice.

"Yes, hello." The young girl giggled. "You are in the Kingdom of Aksum, the oldest African kingdom to ever exist. My name is Aida, which in the Ethiopian language of Amharic means happiness, and this is Maaza," explained the young girl as she pointed to herself and then to the friendly giraffe.

"Nice to meet you both, Aida and Maaza. My name is Ashanti," said Ashanti. "Are we in Ethiopia?"

"Well, something like that," Aida responded. "We are in the Kingdom of Aksum, which is in the northern part of Ethiopia."

Ashanti took a moment to look around and capture the beautiful landscape so she could tell her brother later. There were so many hills and terraces built around for farming and irrigation. Merchants bought and sold goods off in the far distance.

Ashanti thought, "The people that live here must be really advanced." But what caught her attention the most was right in front of her.

"Can you please explain the purpose of this pillar?" Ashanti asked as she turned and pointed to the extremely large structure in front of them.

"Why of course," Maaza responded with flowers gently falling from his head.

"Standing in front of you is King Ezana's stela. It is the great Obelisk of Axum. This is where past leaders are buried, and it stands as a symbol of Aksum's strength." The giraffe sounded like he admired it a lot.

Ashanti looked closer and could see that there was writing on the obelisk. The year inscribed on the monument was from the first century. "That must mean the people here have their own written language," Ashanti thought.

"Of course, we do, our alphabet is called Ge'ez." Maaza responded while opening and closing his big eyes. Ashanti quickly realized she was having a conversation with a talking giraffe.

Back at home, in the kitchen, Kamari jumps out of his chair and puts one hand on his hip as he interrupts his sister's story.

"What in the world? The giraffe spoke to you? What an awesome dream!" he shouts. Kamari interrupts his sister's story one more time by asking, "Do you mean the pillar was high in the sky like an Egyptian pyramid? Those are pretty high up,"

"Yes, exactly," Ashanti says. "But guess what?" Ashanti challenges her brother with her newly gained information. "According to Aida and Maaza, the Aksum Empire was created before the great Egypt civilization. In fact, the ancient Egyptians might have copied the Axumites when they built their pyramids and other monuments."

Before Ashanti can continue her story, Kamari interjects and says, "Okay, so you mean this place existed before Egypt?

Keep telling me more about your dream and the ancient Kingdom of Aksum." His head tilts slightly.

Ashanti is eager to learn more about her distant travel and continues to recall her dream to the place where she began to ask Aida more questions.

"What do people do here?" she'd asked.

Aida smiled. "Here in the Kingdom of Aksum, people work every day. There are farmers. Some people raise cattle while many more people trade. They trade with people from outside lands as far as Rome, Persia, and even India. Here in Aksum, we even have our own currency." Aida sounded proud.

"Look, this is how we often buy goods from other places," she said as she pulled out a gold coin from her satchel she wore across her chest.

Ashanti looked closely at the gold coin that had a design around the outer edge and what looked to be two feathers joining with a picture of a man's head.

"Oh my goodness!" Exclaimed Ashanti. "You mean that the ancient Ethiopian people have their own money?" She couldn't believe it.

"Yes, we are only one of four places in the world that actually have a monetary currency. We are able to have a currency because our African land is rich in gold and iron." Aida explained.

She then reached out her arm to give Ashanti the golden coin she had in her hand. "Please take this. You seem very curious about our land. Would you like to meet the king and queen? I can take you there in just a few minutes. The chariot will be on its way."

Ashanti could not believe her ears. "Who is this girl?" Ashanti wondered. "How could she take me to see the king and queen? How could she have a chariot on standby? Could Aida be a royal princess? And do all animals here talk?"

Overwhelmed with excitement, Ashanti began to jump up and down. "Yes, Aida, yes! I would love to meet them. My brother will never believe this." Trying to maintain her composure, Ashanti looked down and realized she was in her pajamas. Ashanti gasped. "Oh no! I am not properly dressed to meet royal people," Ashanti thought.

Before Ashanti could ask any more questions, her eyes grew heavy and tired and her body got in a tranquil mode. Before she knew it, she was back in her bed fast asleep. Her dream had quickly ended.

"Wow, did you say oldest empire?" asks Kamari after the end of the story. "I thought the only empire that existed in Africa was the Egyptian empire."

Kamari has a confused look on his face and a slight sense of uncertainty. He stares intensely at his sister, looking for clarification.

"Wait a minute. I will be right back!" Ashanti shrieks. Ashanti pushes her chair back from the table and runs up to her bedroom. She grabs something from underneath her pillow. Ashanti returns to the kitchen to find her brother sneaking a strawberry from her plate.

With a guilty look on his face, Kamari grins and says, "I thought you were finished eating breakfast. Anyway, you take way too long to eat your food."

Ignoring the fact that her brother has eaten all his food and now some of hers, she shakes her head and sits back down across the table from him.

Ashanti has one more trick up her sleeve to convince her brother. Without hesitation, Ashanti pulls a gold coin out of her pocket and says, **"Bam!"**

She holds the foreign object up to Kamari's eyes. "Now do you believe me?" Ashanti asks confidently.

She grins as she puts her elbows on the table and rests her chin on her hands and leans in towards her brother.

For the first time all morning, Kamari is speechless. He takes a deep breath and says,

"Um, well … ok, Ashanti. You probably got that coin from an old game set we have in the basement. But anyway, I want to hear the rest of your dream even though I am not totally convinced that there were kings and queens in Africa other than in ancient Egypt. Boy, I sure hope when I am twelve, I can be as smart as you."

Raising both his arms in the air, Kamari says, "So, what happens, what happens next in your dream?"

"Ugh!" Ashanti sighs as she lowers her head. Not wanting to disappoint her little brother, she mumbles as she looks down at her half-eaten breakfast,

"I woke up."

"Oh, don't worry, Ashanti.
I am sure you will remember the rest soon."
Kamari reassures her as he reaches over to hug his sister.

"Don't be sad, you are the best dream teller ever! Hurry up and let's get ready to go to the museum. **Yippie!**"

Words to Know:

Cowrie – A shiny shell with different patterns that's used to trade goods in parts of Africa and Asia.

Ghana – Western African Empire that grew rich from the trade. Ghana is also a present day country in West Africa.

Ethiopia – Eastern African country famous for originating the coffee bean, also gold. It's the only African country never to be colonized or taken over by a European country.

Aksum – One of the greatest African kingdoms of all times. It is located in East Africa. It's known for trade between India and Europe. Aksum was also known for Christianity.

Ge'ez – Aksum had its own alphabet or script.

Amharic – Early Ethiopian language.

Stela – An upright stone slab that was marked as a gravestone generally to remember important people.

Obelisk – A stone pillar with a pointed top.

Irrigation – The process of controlling water to help grow crops.

Axumites – Another name for the Kingdom of Aksum.

Pyramid — A large structure with a triangular shape that was often made as tombs for important people, such as pharaohs in Ancient Egypt.

Currency — Something that is used to exchange one thing for something else. We use money as our currency to buy things we want.

Satchel — A small bag carried on shoulder or across one's chest.

Savannah — An area in Africa with tall grass, exotic animals, and warm temperatures.

Gelada baboon — These animals are from the monkey family. They have a lot of hair around their faces and a red patch underneath their necks and on their chests. They love to talk to each other and spend a lot of time with their families.

Menelik's bushbuck — These animals only live in Ethiopia. They are normally small and look like goats with horns, except they have white stripes across their chest. Menelik was a famous Ethiopian king during the late 1800's.

Mountain nyala — This animal has its picture on Ethiopia's ten-cent coin. Nyalas are very important to the Ethiopian culture. They look like large goats with twisted horns.

Black lion — This lion looks very similar to other lions, but the black lion lives in Ethiopia and has black hair at the end of its mane.